Here's what kids have to say to
Mary Pope Osborne, author of
the Magic Tree House series:

I never ever read that much until I read the Magic Tree House books, and after I read your books, I got started on reading. I read more and more. . . . Keep on writing, and I will keep on reading.—Seth L.

I had one of your books and I couldn't put it down!!! I really, really love your books.—Liza F.

I'm really enjoying your Magic Tree House books. They are my favorite books. . . . Today I had to write about three people I want to have come over for dinner. The three people I chose are Thomas Jefferson, Nicolas Cage, and, you guessed it, Mary Pope Osborne.—Will B.

I have read every single book you've written. . . . I love your books so much I would go wacko if you stopped writing your books.—Stephanie Z.

Once I start one [of your books], I never put it down until it is done. Your books make me feel like I am really in the place that Jack and Annie are in. When I read one of your books, I learn so many interesting new facts. Your books are the best!—Eliza D.

Parents and teachers love
Magic Tree House books, too!

Since we are doing a unit on solar systems I chose <u>Midnight on the Moon</u> (Magic Tree House #8). To my delight, this reading turned out to be the most successful thing I've done this year.
—M. Mishkin

Thank you for providing a series of books for children that are mesmerizing, entertaining, and filled with factual information.
—L. Shlansky

My daughter loves to have me read Magic Tree House stories. She's even been known to sleep with one under her pillow!—E. Becker

What a wonderful series you have created! I have even developed a reading program for my more advanced readers centered around your books. The results have been incredible.
—L. Carpenter

The balance between a sophisticated topic and an easy-to-read book is a hard one to find. Thank you for doing it so well.—A. Doolittle

Dear Readers,

Some time ago, I wrote a biography of George Washington. While doing my research for that book, I began to greatly admire him. Ever since, I've wanted to "visit" him again. Happily, <u>Revolutionary War on Wednesday</u> finally gave me the chance to do just that.

Sal Murdocca, the wonderful artist for the Magic Tree House series, and I thought it would be fun to model our cover after one of America's most famous paintings: <u>Washington Crossing the Delaware</u>, painted by Emanuel Leutze in Germany in 1851. This huge painting now hangs in the Metropolitan Museum of Art in New York City.

We'd like to point out several errors in Leutze's painting (and our cover!), however. First, a general would never have stood up on a rough ride like that. Second, the boat in the painting is much smaller than the ones Washington actually used. And third, the first American flag with thirteen stars, representing the thirteen colonies, was not actually designed until some time _after_ Washington crossed the Delaware.

Still, we love the painting and thought it would be fun to put Jack and Annie into it for our cover.

Have a good time on your journey with Jack, Annie, and George Washington. Just remember—don't stand up in the boat!

All my best,

Mary Pope Osborne

MAGIC TREE HOUSE® #22

Revolutionary War on Wednesday

by Mary Pope Osborne

illustrated by Sal Murdocca

A STEPPING STONE BOOK™

Random House 🏠 New York

For the Foley family—
John, Susie, Jack, and Elliot

Text copyright © 2000 by Mary Pope Osborne.
Illustrations copyright © 2000 by Sal Murdocca.

All rights reserved under International and Pan-American
Copyright Conventions. Published in the United States by
Random House, Inc., New York, and simultaneously in Canada
by Random House of Canada Limited, Toronto.

www.randomhouse.com/kids/magictreehouse

Library of Congress Cataloging-in-Publication Data
Osborne, Mary Pope.
Revolutionary War on Wednesday / by Mary Pope Osborne ;
illustrated by Sal Murdocca.
p. cm. — (Magic tree house series ; #22) "A Stepping Stone book."
SUMMARY: Using their magic tree house, Jack and Annie travel back to the
time of the American Revolution and help General George Washington
during his famous crossing of the Delaware River.
ISBN 978-0-679-89068-3 (trade) — ISBN 978-0-679-99068-0 (lib. bdg.)
[1. Time travel—Fiction. 2. Magic—Fiction.
3. United States—History—Revolution, 1775–1783—Fiction.
4. Washington, George, 1732–1799—Fiction. 5. Tree houses—Fiction.]
I. Murdocca, Sal, ill. II. Title. PZ7.O81167 Re 2000 [Fic]—dc21 00-037299

Printed in the United States of America   September 2000
40 39 38

Random House, Inc.   New York, Toronto, London, Sydney, Auckland

Contents

Prologue

One summer day in Frog Creek, Pennsylvania, a mysterious tree house appeared in the woods.

Eight-year-old Jack and his seven-year-old sister, Annie, climbed into the tree house. They found that it was filled with books.

Jack and Annie soon discovered that the tree house was magic. It could take them to the places in the books. All they had to do was point to a picture and wish to go there.

Along the way, Jack and Annie discovered

that the tree house belongs to Morgan le Fay. Morgan is a magical librarian from Camelot, the long-ago kingdom of King Arthur. She travels through time and space, gathering books.

In Magic Tree House Books #5–8, Jack and Annie helped free Morgan from a spell. In Books #9–12, they solved four ancient riddles and became Master Librarians.

In Magic Tree House Books #13–16, Jack and Annie had to save four ancient stories from being lost forever.

In Magic Tree House Books #17–20, Jack and Annie freed a mysterious little dog from a magic spell.

In Magic Tree House Books #21–24, Jack and Annie have a new challenge. They must find four special kinds of writing for Morgan's library to help save Camelot. They are about to set off to find the second of these . . .

1

Wednesday!

"Wake up, Jack!" Annie whispered.

Jack opened his eyes. He looked at his clock. It was six A.M.

"Come on!" Annie whispered. She was standing at his bedroom door, already dressed.

"Now?" said Jack.

"Yeah, it's Wednesday! We have to go to the tree house!" she said.

"Oh, man, Wednesday!" said Jack. Suddenly, he was wide awake.

"We have to help save Camelot," said
Annie.

"I know, I know," said Jack, scrambling
out of bed.

"Meet you out front," said Annie.

Jack quickly changed into his jeans and

T-shirt. He threw his notebook and pencil into his backpack.

Then he slipped down the stairs and out the front door.

Annie was waiting in the gray early light.

"All set?" she whispered.

"Yep," said Jack.

They took off running across their yard. They ran down their quiet street and into the Frog Creek woods.

Soon they came to the tree house. They climbed up the rope ladder.

In the early light, they saw Morgan's note, the same note they'd found on Sunday. Jack picked it up and read aloud:

Dear Jack and Annie,

Camelot is in trouble. To save the kingdom, please find these four special kinds of writing for my library:

Something to follow
Something to send
Something to learn
Something to lend

Thank you,
Morgan

Annie picked up a piece of paper lying on the floor. It was a list of rules from the famous nurse Clara Barton. They had met her on their journey to the Civil War.

"On Sunday we found the first special writing," said Annie, "*something to follow.*"

"Yeah," said Jack, "and now we need to find the second thing, *something to send.*"

He picked up a book lying near the note. The cover showed soldiers on a snowy riverbank.

The title was *The Revolutionary War.*

Jack frowned.

"Uh-oh," said Annie.

"Another war," said Jack, sighing.

"You still want to go?" said Annie.

"We have to," said Jack. He hated the suffering he'd seen in the Civil War. But they had no choice. They *had* to help Morgan and save Camelot.

He pointed at the cover of the book.

"I wish we could go there," Jack said.

The wind started to blow.

The tree house started to spin.

It spun faster and faster.

Then everything was still.

Absolutely still.

2

Day or Night?

Jack shivered. The wind blew hard.

"It's cold," he said. He could see his breath in the air.

"Wrap your scarf tighter," said Annie.

Jack looked down. He had a wool scarf around his neck.

He was also wearing woolen pants that buttoned at the knees, a coat, and a hat with three corners. On his feet were funny-looking

shoes with buckles. In place of his backpack was a leather bag.

Annie was wearing a long coat over a long dress.

Jack pulled his scarf tighter. Then he looked out the window with Annie.

They'd landed in trees near an icy river. The sky was gray and heavy with clouds.

"It's almost day—or almost night. I can't tell," said Annie.

"Yeah. I hope it's almost day," said Jack.

"I wonder where we'll find *something to send?*" said Annie.

Jack shrugged.

"First we have to find the Revolutionary War," he said.

He opened their research book. By the gray light, he read:

> Over 200 years ago, the United States was made up of thirteen colonies ruled by Britain. From 1775 until 1782, American "patriots" fought for independence from Britain. This was called the Revolutionary War.

Jack took out his notebook. He wrote:

American patriots fight for
independence from Britain

Jack turned the page. There was a picture of soldiers in red uniforms. He read aloud:

> During the Revolutionary War, British soldiers wore red uniforms. For this reason, they were called "redcoats."

Jack wrote in his notebook:

British = redcoats

"Wow, snow," said Annie.

Jack looked up from his writing. Annie was holding her hand out the window. A few snowflakes blew into the tree house.

"Not much yet," said Jack. "But we better find the special writing soon."

"Well, stop reading and come on," said

Annie. She buttoned up her coat and started down the ladder.

"Okay, okay," said Jack. He packed the research book and his notebook into his bag. Then he followed Annie.

When they stepped onto the ground, there were more snow flurries. The sky was growing darker.

"I'm afraid it's almost night instead of day," said Jack.

"Yeah," said Annie, looking around. "Hey, look—people."

She pointed up the river. In the misty distance was a campfire. Several men sat around the fire. They all held muskets.

"Maybe they can help us," said Annie. She started away. But Jack grabbed her.

"Wait, I think they're soldiers," he said.

"They have muskets. Remember the muskets from the Civil War? The guns that the soldiers carried?"

"Oh, yeah," said Annie.

"They might be redcoats," said Jack. "Let's sneak closer and get a better look at their uniforms."

"Quick," said Annie, "before it's too dark to see."

3

It's Time

Annie lifted up her long dress and ran to a tree close to the river. Jack held on to his hat and ran after her.

They peeked out from behind the tree. More snow flurries swirled in the twilight.

"Redcoats?" whispered Annie.

"Can't tell," said Jack.

In the flickering firelight, the men didn't seem to be wearing uniforms at all. They wore ragged pants and coats. Some even had their feet wrapped in tattered cloth.

"Come on," Annie said.

She ran to a tree closer to the river.

Jack followed.

"This is as close as we should get," he whispered.

"But we still can't tell what they're wearing," said Annie.

She crept forward and hid behind a scraggly bush.

"No closer!" Jack whispered.

But Annie took off again. She crouched behind a rock. She was only about ten feet from the campfire.

Oh, brother, she's way too close now, Jack thought.

But he took a deep breath and ran to the rock.

When he joined Annie, she looked at him and grinned.

"This is like hide-and-seek," she whispered.

"It's not a game, Annie," Jack whispered back. "It's *war*. Be serious."

"I *am* serious!" said Annie, her voice rising.

"Shh!" said Jack.

But it was too late. One of the men stood up and looked around.

"What's the matter, Captain?" another asked.

"I heard something," said the captain. He held up his musket.

Jack stopped breathing.

"Who's there?" the captain shouted.

Jack looked at Annie. She shrugged.

"We're caught," she whispered.

"Who's there?" the captain shouted again.

"Just two kids," Annie answered in a small voice.

"Come out and show yourselves!" the captain said.

Jack and Annie stood up from behind the rock. They both held up their hands.

"We come in peace," said Annie.

In the shadowy twilight, the captain moved toward them.

"Who are you?" he asked.

"We're Jack and Annie," said Annie.

"Why were you spying on us?" he asked.

"We weren't spying," said Jack. "We just wanted to know if you were redcoats or patriots."

"Which would you like us to be?" the shadowy figure asked.

"Patriots," said Jack.

"We *are* patriots," the captain said.

"Thank goodness!" said Annie.

The captain smiled.

"Where are you from?" he asked. His voice had softened.

"We're visiting relatives nearby," Jack said.

"Frog Creek, Pennsylvania," said Annie at the same time.

"But that's amazing!" the captain said. "My farm is in Frog Creek. Where is your farm?"

Jack didn't know how to answer.

"It's near the Frog Creek woods," said Annie.

"All farms are near woods," the man said with a laugh. "What—"

Just then, someone called from up the river. "It's time, Captain!"

The captain turned to the other men near the campfire. "It's time!" he repeated.

The soldiers quickly put out their fire. They stood with their muskets on their shoulders.

"Time for what, Captain?" Annie asked.

"Time to meet up with our commander-in-chief," he said. "Return to your family now so your mother and father won't worry about you."

"Yes, sir," said Jack.

"It is nice to see children," the captain said. "I was just trying to write a letter to my own son and daughter. I didn't know what to say."

"Tell them that you miss them," said Annie.

The man smiled.

"And I do, indeed," he said softly.

Then he turned and headed up the river-bank. His ragged men followed behind. Soon they all disappeared into the cold mist.

Jack looked around. The wind was blowing harder. The snow was sticking to the ground.

"What now?" he asked.

More than anything, he wanted to go back

home. With the soldiers gone, the riverbank felt lonely and scary.

"We still have to find *something to send*," said Annie.

"I know," said Jack.

"Maybe we should just follow the captain and his men," said Annie. "They might lead us to something."

Jack wasn't sure that was a good idea. But he didn't have a better one.

"Okay. But let's try not to get caught this time," he said.

He and Annie took off through the frozen twilight, following the snowy footprints of the American patriots.

4

Commander-in-Chief

Jack and Annie ran along the riverbank. The wind whooshed over the cold water. Wet snowflakes hissed in the dark.

But then Jack heard other sounds. He heard voices, lots of voices.

He and Annie soon came upon hundreds and hundreds of soldiers gathered near the dark river.

Many carried oil lanterns. The lanterns gave an eerie glow to the snowy twilight.

"The captain and his men must be here somewhere," said Jack, looking around.

Boats like giant canoes were tied near the river. Men were leading horses and loading cannons onto the boats.

"What are they all doing?" said Annie.

Jack pulled out their Revolutionary War book. He read in a whisper:

On Wednesday, December 25, 1776—

"December 25? That's Christmas!" said Annie. "Today's Christmas!"

"Cool," said Jack. He started reading again:

> **On Wednesday, December 25, 1776, the patriots were losing the war. Ragged and weary, many were ready to give up. Then something began to**

**happen that would turn the war
around. About 2,400 American
patriots gathered on the west bank
of the Delaware River in Pennsylvania.
They prepared to cross the river to go
on a secret mission.**

"A *secret* mission? Oh, man . . . ," said Jack. He started to pull out his notebook.

"Attention, troops! The commander-in-chief!" a soldier shouted.

Jack and Annie saw a man in a dark cape and a three-cornered hat ride up on a white horse.

The commander-in-chief loomed above the crowd of soldiers. His cape flapped in the wind.

He sat calmly and with dignity on the back of his horse.

Even at a distance, Jack thought the commander-in-chief looked familiar, *very* familiar. But he couldn't figure out why.

"A dangerous mission lies before you all," the man shouted above the wind. "But I want you to have courage. You must remember the words of Thomas Paine."

The commander-in-chief held up a piece of paper. He read to his men:

"'These are the times that try men's souls. The summer soldier and the sunshine patriot will, in this crisis, shrink from the service of their country. But he that stands it now deserves the love and thanks of man and woman. . . .'"

"Wow, that's great," whispered Annie.

Listening to the powerful words, Jack felt his spirits rise, too.

"'The harder the conflict, the more glorious the triumph,'" the commander-in-chief read on. "'What we obtain too cheap, we esteem too lightly. It is dearness only that gives everything its value.'"

There was a silence, as if everyone were thinking about the words the man had read. Then the soldiers started cheering and clapping. They didn't seem tired at all anymore.

Now they seemed eager to set out on their mission.

The commander-in-chief saluted his men. He steered his horse toward the river.

As the horse moved past them, Jack got a better look at the rider.

He gasped.

Of course! he thought. He'd seen that face before—on dollar bills!

Jack grabbed Annie's arm.

"I know who the commander-in-chief is!" he exclaimed. "He's *George Washington!*"

5

The Letter

"George Washington? Really?" said Annie.

"Yeah, I think he is!" said Jack.

"Wow! Where'd he go?" said Annie. "I want to see him again! Come on!"

She started toward the river.

"Wait—don't go far," said Jack. "I just want to make sure it's him."

He opened the Revolutionary War book. He found a picture of the boats on the riverbank. He read:

When General George Washington gathered his troops by the Delaware River, he was commander-in-chief of the whole American army. The general led the army for six years, until America became a free and independent nation. In 1789, he was elected the first president of the new United States.

"Oh, man, it *is* him," said Jack.

He pulled out his notebook and wrote:

General George Washington helped America become independent

"Hey, what are you writing?" someone asked.

Jack looked up.

A bearded soldier was pointing at him.

Jack shoved the Revolutionary War book

and his notebook into his bag.

"Nothing, sir," he said. He started walking away.

The man shouted after Jack. But Jack ran down toward the river and lost himself in a crowd of soldiers.

When he looked over his shoulder, he was relieved. The bearded man was nowhere in sight.

"Stop, young man!" Someone shone a lantern right in Jack's face.

Jack gasped.

It was the captain.

"I told you to go home, Jack," the captain said sternly. "Where's your sister?"

Jack looked around. Where *was* Annie?

"I don't know," he said.

"Find her at once and go back to your family!" the captain ordered. "Our secret mission is very important. Children will only get in the way."

"Yes, sir!" said Jack.

The captain started to leave. But he stopped.

"I wonder if you could do me a favor, Jack?" he asked.

"Sure," said Jack.

The captain pulled out his letter.

"This is my letter to my children," he said. "It's a farewell letter. Would you please take it back with you to Frog Creek?"

"Yes, sir," said Jack.

"You must only send it if you hear that we have failed in our mission and many patriots were lost," said the captain.

"Yes, sir," said Jack.

The captain handed his letter to Jack.

"I copied the general's speech for my children," the captain said. "If anything bad happens to me, I hope those words will give them courage."

The captain then turned and disappeared into the crowd.

"Good luck, Captain!" Jack called. He hoped he would never have to send the letter to the man's children.

Suddenly, Jack clutched the letter to his chest.

"*Send!*" he whispered.

This letter was the writing they'd been looking for—*something to send!* He and Annie could go home now! Their mission was over!

Jack shoved the captain's letter into his

bag. Now he just had to find Annie.

As he looked around, he shivered.

"Where is she?" he muttered.

Jack started moving through the crowd, looking for Annie.

It was hard to see. The wind was blowing harder. The snow fell faster.

Jack started to panic.

"Annie!" he called.

As he wove quickly in and out of the crowd, he kept calling for her. None of the soldiers noticed him. They were all too busy.

Finally, Jack came to the river.

Through the lamplit mist, he saw soldiers waiting to get into the boats. Some had already climbed aboard.

"Jack!" came a cry.

Jack saw the figure of a small girl. She

was sitting in the back of the biggest boat.

"No way," he whispered.

Jack charged down to the boat. He stood at the edge of the water.

"What are you doing?" Jack shouted.

"This is George Washington's boat," Annie said. "It's our big chance to spend time with him! We might not get another one."

Jack looked at the other end of the huge boat. Through the mist and falling snow, he saw the commander-in-chief talking to his crew.

"We can't go with him," said Jack. "We'll get in the way of his secret mission. Besides, we have *something to send* now!"

"What? How?" said Annie.

"A letter! The captain gave me his letter to take back to Frog Creek!" said Jack.

"We're only supposed to send it if something bad happens to the captain. We can go home now!"

"Oh, can't we go a little later?" Annie asked.

Jack climbed into the boat to pull her out.

"No, come on," he said, taking her hand.

Suddenly, the crew moved to the back of the boat, near Jack and Annie. The men grabbed their oars and started pushing the boat away from the shore.

"We're taking off," said Annie.

"No! We have to get out!" Jack said to the rowers.

But the men were working too hard to pay attention. They were using their oars to hack up the ice at the edge of the river.

"Excuse me," Jack said in a loud voice.

Just then, the boat jolted forward. Jack nearly lost his balance.

The boat broke through more ice. Rough waves sloshed against its sides.

"We have to go back!" said Jack.

"Too late," said Annie.

They were headed across the Delaware River!

6

Crossing the Delaware

The huge boat rocked in the water. Giant chunks of ice smashed against its sides.

"Thanks *a lot*, Annie," Jack whispered. He shivered in the snowy cold. "We're not supposed to go on their secret mission with them."

"It's okay," she whispered. "Maybe we can help George Washington."

"Are you nuts?" Jack whispered. "We should be on our way home now."

The boat hit a piece of ice. The boat bounced, then dipped into the river.

Jack clung to the wooden side. He hoped they wouldn't turn over. *Nobody could survive in this icy water*, he thought. It would be like sinking on the *Titanic*.

The crew fought hard to keep the boat moving forward. They rowed past chunks of ice into a smoother part of the river.

Light from oil lamps shone on the water, making the ice chunks behind them glow like huge, glittering jewels.

Jack looked back. Other boats were following them. They were filled with soldiers, horses, and cannons.

"Where exactly are we going?" Annie whispered.

Jack shrugged. He reached into his bag

and pulled out their Revolutionary War book.

By the dim lantern light in the boat, he searched through the book. He found a painting of General Washington crossing the Delaware River.

He showed the painting to Annie. They each read the caption silently:

> After George Washington crossed the Delaware, he led his men on a nine-mile march to a British post. The post was filled with Hessians, German soldiers hired by the British to fight for them. The American patriots caught them off guard. The Hessians never thought the patriots would attack on a stormy Christmas night. It was a great victory for the patriots. They captured almost 1,000 Hessians. Hardly any of Washington's men were lost.

"Yay! We won't have to send the captain's letter!" Annie exclaimed.

"Shh!" said Jack.

But George Washington turned around and looked back at Jack and Annie.

Oh, no, Jack thought, *caught again.*

He closed his eyes, as if that would make him invisible.

"He's coming," said Annie.

Jack looked up.

George Washington was making his way back toward them.

In the next moment, the commander-in-chief loomed above them like a giant shadow.

"Children?" he asked in a quiet, angry voice.

"Sorry," Jack squeaked.

"Merry Christmas!" said Annie.

But George Washington did not say "Merry Christmas" back.

7

Spies!

"What are you doing here?" George Washington asked. The commander-in-chief sounded furious.

"We made a mistake," Jack said. "We—we didn't mean to come."

George Washington turned to the rowers.

"Who let these children sneak aboard?" he asked in a stern voice.

The men looked at Jack and Annie with surprise.

"It's not their fault," Annie said quickly. "They were working too hard to notice us."

Just then, the boat banged against the ice. The ice cracked. The boat moved on, then bumped against the shore.

Two soldiers jumped out and pulled the boat up on the shore.

George Washington looked at Jack and Annie.

"This boat is returning to get more men," he said. "When it does, you two will get out and stay on the other shore."

"Yes, sir," said Jack. He felt very embarrassed.

George Washington then gave orders to the rowers.

"Make sure these children do *not* board any other boats when you return," he said.

The general stepped onto the riverbank.

The wind started to pick up. The snow fell harder. As the crew unloaded the boat, neither Jack nor Annie spoke.

Jack was miserable. They had caused trouble for George Washington—just when the general was trying to make America an independent nation.

Jack desperately wished he and Annie had gone home earlier.

They watched more and more boats land on the riverbank. As the soldiers unloaded their weapons and horses, a freezing rain began. Now rain, snow, and sleet fell together.

Jack heard George Washington call to one of his men.

"This storm is getting worse, Major!" the general said.

"Yes, sir!" the major said.

"I think we're in for a blizzard," said Washington.

"Yes, sir! Our mission may be hopeless, sir," said the major. "Should we call it off?"

"No, you shouldn't," Jack whispered. "You're going to win."

"Should we turn back, sir?" the major said.

"No, no!" said Annie.

She stood up. The boat rocked.

"Don't turn back, George Washington, sir!" she shouted. "You have to march on, sir! You have to attack the Hessians, sir!"

"Shh!" Jack tried to pull Annie back down. "We're not supposed to know about their secret mission!"

"How does she know our plans, Major?" George Washington asked.

"Listen to us, sir!" said Annie. "You're going to win!" She pulled away from Jack and jumped out of the boat.

"Annie!" Jack leaped onto the riverbank. He scrambled after Annie up the steep, icy slope.

"You have to lead your men, General Washington, sir!" Annie said. "The Hessians will be surprised! They think no army will be marching on a night like this!"

"How do you know all this?" the major shouted above the storm. "How do you know what the Hessians are doing and thinking?"

"I—I—" For once, Annie seemed at a loss for words.

"She just guessed!" said Jack.

Just then, the bearded soldier who had yelled at Jack earlier stepped forward.

"I saw this boy earlier," he said. "He was writing things down."

"No, I was just . . ." Now Jack was at a loss for words.

"Seize them!" the major shouted. "They're spies!"

8

These Are the Times

Jack grabbed Annie's hand.

"We're *not* spies!" he said.

He whirled around to face George Washington.

"General Washington, remember those words you said to your men?" Jack said. "You should believe them yourself, sir!"

"What are you talking about?" George Washington asked.

Jack yanked the captain's letter from his bag.

By the light of the lamp, he read the words the captain had copied for his children:

"'These are the times that try men's souls . . . ,'" Jack read. "'But he that stands it now deserves the love and thanks of man and woman. . . . The harder the conflict, the more glorious the triumph.'"

Jack looked at George Washington.

"Even if things look impossible, you should keep going, sir," he said. "The harder things seem, the greater the triumph, right? That's what you read to your men. You have to keep going for *their* sake."

"Yes! And you have to keep going for *our* sake," said Annie. "For the sake of the *future* children of America, sir."

As the wet snow hissed about them, George Washington stared a long moment at Jack and Annie.

Finally, he put a hand on each of their shoulders.

"I do not know who you are," he said. "I do not know how you know what you know. But I believe you. For your sake, and for the future children of America, we *will* march on."

"Yay!" cried Annie.

"Yay," said Jack softly. He sighed with relief and put away the captain's letter.

"Now get back in the boat," said George Washington. "You must leave the fighting to us. To me and my men."

Jack felt very grateful to George Washington and his whole army. They were risking their lives for all of America's children, past and future. He could barely speak.

"Thank you, sir," said Annie.

"Thank you both for telling me to listen to my own advice," said George Washington. He called to the rowers waiting in the boat. "Take good care of these two."

George Washington climbed onto his horse. He looked down at Jack and Annie.

"Merry Christmas," he said.

Then the commander-in-chief rode away into the stormy darkness.

9

Flash!

"All aboard!" one of the rowers called.

Jack and Annie hurried down the steep riverbank. They climbed back into the boat.

The crew pushed away from the shore. The boat started back through the icy, churning waters of the Delaware River.

Jack was freezing in the sleet and snow. But he didn't worry about that now. He was thinking instead about how they had helped George Washington. He was thinking about how they had helped keep history on its course.

Jack felt great.

When they got to the riverbank, Jack and Annie jumped out of the boat.

"Thanks!" Jack yelled to the rowers.

With the wind at their backs, Jack and Annie took off through the blizzard. They ran down the icy bank of the Delaware River.

Thunder rumbled in the snowy sky.

Lightning zigzagged over the woods.

"How will we find the tree house?" cried Annie.

"I don't know!" said Jack. "But don't worry! We'll find it!"

He felt very confident now, after meeting George Washington. After being *thanked* by George Washington!

He and Annie ran on through the rain and the snow and the sleet.

They ran along the riverbank—until a bright flash of lightning lit up the sky. Then Jack saw it!

The tree house was directly to their left, high in a tall tree covered with snow.

"Over there!" he shouted.

Jack and Annie ran toward the edge of the woods.

In the dark, Jack looked up, searching for the tree house.

Lightning lit the woods again. Jack saw the rope ladder flapping wildly in the wind.

He grabbed it.

"Annie!" he called.

"Here!" she said.

"Let's go!" he said.

They climbed up the swaying ladder and scrambled into the tree house. They were soaking wet and covered with slush and snow.

Annie grabbed the Pennsylvania book.

"I wish we could go there!" she shouted.

The wind blew even harder.

The tree house started to spin.

It spun faster and faster.

Then everything was still.

Absolutely still.

10

This Peaceful Place

Gray early light spilled into the tree house.

Birds sounded in the woods.

The summer wind felt warm and gentle. Jack and Annie were wearing their nice, dry clothes again.

"Oh, man," said Jack. "It's good to be home."

"Yeah," said Annie, sighing, "back in this peaceful place."

Jack pulled the captain's letter out of his

pack. He turned it over. It was addressed to:

Molly and Ben Sanders
Apple Tree Farm
Frog Creek, Pennsylvania

"Molly and Ben lived on a farm near these woods over two hundred years ago," said Jack.

Annie gently touched the letter.

"Your dad is going to make it home, kids. He misses you," Annie whispered, as if she could send comforting words back through time.

Jack carefully placed the special writing from the Revolutionary War next to the writing from the Civil War.

"Look," said Annie. She picked up a note lying in the corner. It said simply: *Come back on Tuesday.*

"Another message from Morgan," said Annie.

Jack smiled.

He pulled on his pack.

"See you on Tuesday, tree house," he said.

He started down the rope ladder. Annie followed.

In the early daylight, they ran through the Frog Creek woods. Then they ran down their street.

They climbed onto their porch and rested against the railing. They looked out at the dawn sky.

Jack remembered the *whoosh* of the cold wind on the Delaware. He remembered the *hiss* of the wet snow and the *slosh* of the icy waves.

He remembered George Washington reading to his men.

"The harder the conflict, the more glorious the triumph," Jack whispered.

"Those words are true," said Annie. "It *was* a hard conflict, and I feel kind of glorious right now. Don't you?"

Jack laughed.

"Yeah, definitely," he said.

Then he and Annie slipped into their quiet, peaceful house.

THE THIRTEEN COLONIES

Long ago, the United States was made up of thirteen small colonies. Many of the early settlers, or colonists, thought of England as their "mother country." They were proud to have come from England, and they felt great loyalty to the British king.

Over time, though, many colonists wanted to be independent. They did not want a faraway country to rule over them. These colonists were called *patriots*.

THE REVOLUTIONARY WAR AND GEORGE WASHINGTON

In the spring of 1775, fighting broke out between the patriots and the British in Lexington and Concord, Massachusetts.

That summer, a group of American

patriots met in Philadelphia and began to organize an army to fight the British. They made George Washington their commander-in-chief.

After the patriots won independence over eight years later, Washington resigned as commander-in-chief. He returned to the life of a gentleman farmer on his plantation in Mount Vernon, Virginia.

Six years later, in 1789, George Washington was elected the first president of the United States.

THOMAS PAINE

At the beginning of the Revolutionary War, some colonists did not want to break away from England. These people were called *Tories*.

In January 1776, a British writer named Thomas Paine wrote a powerful essay that attacked the idea of obeying a king. Paine called his essay *Common Sense*. It inspired many Tories to join the patriots' cause.

Almost a year later, in December 1776, George Washington's army was losing the war. Many soldiers wanted to give up. This time Thomas Paine wrote a series of essays called *The Crisis*.

George Washington had *The Crisis* read aloud to his troops on the banks of the Delaware River.

Paine's words inspired the troops to continue the fight. They crossed the Delaware River, defeated the enemy, and gave new hope to the whole patriot army.

Want to learn more about the American Revolution?

Get the facts behind the fiction in the Magic Tree House® Research Guide.

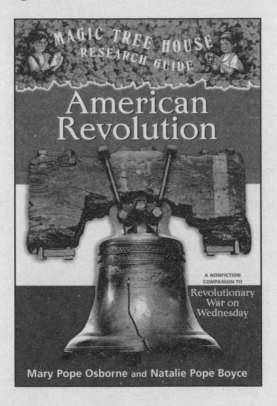

Available now!

Have you read the Magic Tree House book in which Jack and Annie go on their most important mission yet?

MAGIC TREE HOUSE® #21

CIVIL WAR ON SUNDAY

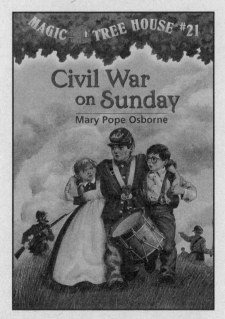

Don't miss the next Magic Tree House book,
in which Jack and Annie are whisked
back to a prairie in the 1870s, where
danger is a part of everyday life!

MAGIC TREE HOUSE® #23

TWISTER ON TUESDAY

340

Are you a fan of the Magic Tree House® series?

Visit our
MAGIC TREE HOUSE®
Web site
at

www.magictreehouse.com

Exciting sneak previews of the next book.
Games, puzzles, and other fun activities.
Contests with super prizes.
And much more!